TERRY DEARY'S
GREEK TALES

THE LION'S SLAVE

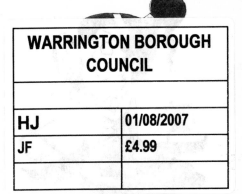

Illustrated by Helen Flook

A & C Black • London

First published 2007 by
A & C Black Publishers Ltd
38 Soho Square, London, W1D 3HB

www.acblack.com

Text copyright © 2007 Terry Deary
Illustrations copyright © 2007 Helen Flook

The rights of Terry Deary and Helen Flook to be identified as the
author and illustrator of this work have been asserted by them in
accordance with the Copyrights, Designs and Patents Act 1988.

ISBN 978-0-7136-8222-9

A CIP catalogue for this book is available from the British Library.

This book is produced using paper that is made from wood grown in
managed, sustainable forests. It is natural, renewable and recyclable.
The logging and manufacturing processes conform to the
environmental regulations of the country of origin.

Printed in Great Britain by CPI Bookmarque, Croydon, CR0 4TD

THE LION'S SLAVE

INTRODUCTION

Syracuse, 213 BC

Aesop the Greek storyteller said:
You may share the work of the great,
but you will not share the rewards.

My master liked to call me stupid. "You are stupid, Lydia," he would say. "If you had twice as many brains, you'd be a half-wit."

That was a clever thing to say. But then my master, Archimedes, was the cleverest man in the whole of Greece. So if he called me stupid, then I must have been.

I cleaned his rooms ...

and washed his clothes ...

cooked his meals ...

and helped him test his machines.

Because Archimedes was a great inventor, they called him the Lion of Syracuse. And he often roared at me like a lion.

"I bet your brain feels as good as new, seeing that you've never used it," he told me.

"Thank you, sir," I said.

And I was clumsy. When I tried to dust the bottles and jars in his workshop, I often spilled them.

"You are a donkey, Lydia. What are you?"

"A donkey, sir," I said.

There was a story about
Archimedes taking a bath one day,
long before I went to work for him.
He lay in the bath and the water
overflowed.

That gave him an idea – some
maths idea I've never understood.
Anyway, Archimedes jumped out of
the bath and ran down the street
calling out the news.

"Eureka*!" he cried. "I have found it! Eureka! I have found the answer!"

But Archimedes hadn't stopped to put on any clothes!

* Of course, you know *eureka* is Ancient Greek for "I have found it". Eureka! was one of Archimedes' favourite cries.

He forgot about simple things like that. And I reckon it was his brilliant brain that got him killed.

He thought everyone was as excited by his inventions as he was. He forgot that people have feelings. Feelings of revenge.

If he'd been as stupid as me then he'd still be alive today.

It all started when the Romans came to Syracuse...

CHAPTER ONE

"You are stupid, Lydia, stupid," Archimedes told me. "I don't know why I hired you. You must be a very cheap servant."

"I am more than cheap, you don't pay me anything at all," I reminded him.

"Then how do you live?"

"I eat a little of the food I cook for you and I sleep on a straw bed in an attic room."

"Huh!" he grumbled. "Then I still pay you too much."

"Yes, sir," I said.

And on that day, the Romans arrived to attack us. Their ships lay in the cool, blue sea off the shore of Syracuse. Soldiers stood on the decks, but didn't dare to land just yet. Our soldiers on the walls would have shot them with their arrows.

"Will the Romans kill us when they land, sir?" I asked.

"Stupid child," Archimides said.  "You, Lydia, are a young and healthy girl. They will not kill you. You are not worth it. They will take you away and make you a slave. But then you will not have a kind master like me, will you?"

"No, sir," I said.

Archimedes' house stood on the top of a hill. We could look over the garden walls and down over the city walls to see the Roman fleet shimmering in the heat. The sun beat down on us and I wished I could swim in that cool, blue sea.

"I would like to smash those ships," Archimedes said.

"You could throw rocks at them," I suggested.

He looked at me and mopped his bald, sweating head with a cloth. "Stupid girl," he said.

"Can you do something about them?" I asked.

"Perhaps I could ... I could invent something," he said.

I clapped my hands and jumped on the dry, brown grass. "That would be marvellous, sir. You are a wonderful inventor. You invented a way to raise water out of a river and into the fields."

"Yes," he nodded. "They call it Archimedes' screw."

"I'm sure you could invent a machine to fire big rocks at those ships," I said.

My master shook his head. "Find me a rock and I'll show you why it's not possible."

There were no rocks in the garden because I kept it weeded and full of flowers. But there were some large ones in the field outside the garden wall.

"I'll get one from the field," I said. Archimedes threw up his hands. "Silly child. Those stones are too large for you to carry."

"Then I'll throw one over the wall," I offered.

"If you can't pick it up, you can't throw it!" He roared his lion roar.

"Oh, throwing it is easier!" I laughed. Then I picked up the plank of wood that my master used as a garden seat, tucked it under my arm and walked out into the field.

I placed the plank on a round stone and let one end drop onto the ground.

I rolled a large rock onto that end. Then I jumped onto the other end. The rock shot up into the air.

I remember it to this day.

I remember the way my master Archimedes screamed...

CHAPTER TWO

The rock soared into the cloudless
sky, looped over the wall and headed
down into the garden. At least it
would have headed into the garden
if my master hadn't been standing
there. Instead, it sort of headed for
his head.

Handsome young Ajax, who lives in the main street, has fine hair that is parted in the middle. My master doesn't have hair on his head. If he *had*, the  rock would have parted it. Instead, it almost parted his head – and then all those fine brains would have spilled out onto the dusty grass and spoiled my fine flowers.

But Archimedes ducked and scrambled out of the way and the rock landed with a thump on the grass.

"Oooops!" I said with a silly grin. "Sorry, sir!"

He didn't call me stupid – he was spluttering and moaning too much to call me anything. I brought the plank back into the garden, made it into a seat again and sat him down.

"You ... you..." he began.

"I know," I said. "I'm foolish."

He shook his head. "You ... you ... could ... have..."

"I could have fired a bigger rock and you would have seen it better," I nodded.

He shook his head. "You ... you ... could ... have ... killed me!"

"Sorry, sir. It was a game I played with my brothers when we were younger. We used to use a small plank to fire balls of cloth in the air and see who could catch them. But I knew it would work for a rock, too."

He glared at me. "Why did you do that?" he demanded.

"Because you told me to get you a rock."

"I did?"

"You did."

"So I did! I was going to show you that it's impossible to throw big rocks at the Roman ships," he said.

"If you say so, sir," I muttered.

"But if I get a really long plank..."

"As long as a tree," I said.

"As long as a tree … then I could fire boulders big enough to sink those ships."

I covered my mouth with my hand. "Oh, sir, that's brilliant! Oh, sir, I knew you'd invent something to save us! It's true what they say!"

"What *do* they say?"

"That you are the cleverest man in Syracuse!"

Archimedes smiled and nodded. "I am the cleverest man in Greece. In the *world*, in fact!"

CHAPTER THREE

You know what happened next, of
course. It is written in the history
books. Archimedes made his mighty
throwing machines – he called them
"catapults".

The Lord of Syracuse gathered the crowds in the main square. He himself stood at the window of the palace. "The people of Syracuse are blessed by the gods," he cried. "The Romans have their ships and soldiers, but we have Archimedes ... the Lion of Syracuse!"

And we all cheered till our throats were sore.

"Roman ships have been sunk," the Lord went on (to more cheers), "and the rest have been driven out to sea. All thanks to the great inventor, Archimedes!"

Cheers! More cheers and more.

The next morning, I rose from my straw bed to make my master his breakfast. I found him in the garden, kneeling beside the pond. He was using a toy catapult to fire at toy ships on the pond.

"Would you like breakfast, sir?"
I asked.

He waved me away with a hand.
When he was thinking his great
thoughts, no one else mattered.

"In the night, the Romans sailed
into our harbour under the cloak of
darkness," he said quickly.

"So? We can sink them with your great war machines."

He took a pebble and placed it on the toy catapult. "Look ... there is a Roman ship in the harbour. I fire a rock."

He fired. The rock landed in the middle of the pond and missed the little ship.

"So? We can move the catapult
back!" I said.

"I've tried it, simple girl."

He moved the catapult back.
He fired again. This time the rock
landed on the edge of the pond.

"See?" he groaned. "It landed
on the harbour. If we get it wrong,
we will shatter our own town. The
Romans are clever. They know we
can't fire at them when they are
so close."

I looked at the models and picked up a twig from the garden tree. I took a thread from my tunic and dangled it from the twig. I took a pin and bent it.

"What are you doing, stupid girl?" Archimedes asked.

"When I was a child, I used to fish with my brothers."

I dangled my little rod over the model ship and hooked it into the air. "If the Romans come too close, we could fish them out of the water!" I laughed.

"Idiot child," he snapped. "We cannot build a mighty fishing rod. It's a stupid idea."

"I know, sir," I sighed.

Archimedes snapped his fingers.
"But if we built a tall crane,"
he murmured, taking the rod
from my hand. "We could
reach out over the harbour
and snatch at the Roman ships.
Fix a claw on the end, like
a crab's, and snatch
them! *Eureka*!"

I covered my mouth with my hand. "Oh, sir, that's brilliant! Oh, sir, I knew you'd invent something to save us! It's true what they say!"

"What *do* they say?"

"That you are the cleverest man in Syracuse!"

"We will call it Archimedes' claw!" he nodded.

CHAPTER FOUR

You will know that Archimedes'
claw smashed several Roman ships
and drove them back.

Again, the Lord of Syracuse gathered the people in the square and told them how great my master was. He paid Archimedes a fortune.

It was strange that his great mind took simple ideas and made them work as weapons of war. Simple games that I used to play as a child.

I was too stupid to see how they could help us win the war. But I felt I was sharing in my master's work.

One day, I made a fire using a mirror that bent the sun's rays into a beam of scorching light.

Archimedes watched me and went off muttering.

The next day, my master had built a huge metal mirror that sent a red ray of fire onto the Roman fleet and set their ships alight.

The Lord of Syracuse heaped more treasures on my master. I was so proud of him! I suppose, in a way, that is how I killed him. Well, I didn't take his life *myself*. But I was to blame. I was stupid.

You see, the Romans landed in the end. They ran through the town, slaying and avenging.

Finally, they reached our house at the top of the hill. My master was in the garden, planning something new. He was drawing circles in the dust with a stick.

A Roman soldier came up to the gate. "Who lives here?" he asked.

"My master Archimedes, the Lion of Syracuse," I said proudly. And showed him through the garden to where my master was scratching away.

The soldier sighed. "We've heard about him. General Marcellus said he is not to be harmed."

"Ah!" I said. "That's nice. Especially after all he did to you!"

The soldier went stiff. "Did? What do you mean, *did*? He does science and maths and stuff. Harmless, isn't he?"

"Ha! That's good," I laughed. "The great Archimedes invented the catapult that sank your ships."

"My friend died on one of those ships," the soldier growled and pulled his sword free of its sheath.

"Then he invented Archimedes' claw that wrecked more of your ships," I giggled.

"My brother died on one of those ships," the soldier fumed and raised his sword above his head.

"And of course he invented the burning mirror that scorched the rest," I finished.

"I was burned on the arm by that!" the soldier roared. He stepped towards my master. "Archimedes – villain – come with me!"

My master waved him away with a hand. When he was thinking his great thoughts, no one else mattered. Then he said his famous last words: "Don't disturb my circles".

They were his last words because the soldier brought down his sword with the fury of a madman. He spilt my master's mighty brains over those circles in the dust.

EPILOGUE

I know. I am stupid. I should not
have told an angry soldier that
Archimedes had invented the killing
machines. I should
have said, "*I*
showed my
master how the
catapult worked.
My fishing rod
gave him the idea
for the claw. And
my mirror showed him how to
make a deadly sunbeam."

But the soldier wouldn't believe a stupid girl could do something like that. Or, here's a chilling thought – maybe he *would* have blamed me. Then he would have killed me! Maybe being stupid saved my life!

So that is the story of how the Lion of Syracuse died. But what happened to the lion's slave? What happened to me?

You won't be surprised to hear that my master was right – I became a Roman slave. But it's not such a bad life. My new master is kind. In fact, he's far kinder to me than old Archimedes and he *never* calls me stupid!

I only wish my master had shared some of his riches with me before he died. The Lord of Syracuse gave him a fortune for his clever machines. I got nothing – though sometimes I think I helped create those inventions.

Still, as Aesop said, "You may share the work of the great, but you will not share the rewards."

And here's another thought: master Archimedes' reward was a sword in the head. So maybe I can't complain too much.

It was such a pity though. All those fine lion brains that spilled out onto the dusty grass. His circles were disturbed ... and the killing spoiled my fine flowers, too.

Such a pity.

TERRY DEARY'S
GREEK TALES

THE BOY WHO CRIED HORSE

TROY, 1180 BC

Acheron is the best liar in Troy. In his
stories he can make King Paris and the
Trojan heroes sound like gods. When a
stranger arrives in the city, with news
that the Greek enemy have left without
a fight, Acheron is suspicious. But will
anyone believe his latest story?

Greek Tales are exciting, funny stories based
on historical events – short chapters and
illustrations throughout are perfect for
building reading confidence.

ISBN 978 0 7136 8216 8   £4.99

TERRY DEARY'S
GREEK TALES

THE
TORTOISE
AND THE
DARE

OLYMPIA, GREECE, 776 BC

Ellie is furious – her twin brother Cypselis
has made a bet. If he beats Big Bacchiad in
the school Olympics foot race, their family
will receive a goat, if he loses, she will
become the bully's slave. And with the odds
stacked against him, how can she make sure
Cypselis stands a chance of winning?

Greek Tales are exciting, funny stories based
on historical events – short chapters and
illustrations throughout are perfect for
building reading confidence.

ISBN 978 0 7136 8220 5   £4.99

TERRY DEARY'S
GREEK TALES
THE
TOWN MOUSE
AND THE
SPARTAN HOUSE

ATHENS, GREECE, 430 BC

Athens is at war with Sparta, home to
the cruellest people on Earth. But when
plague spreads through the city, Darius
is forced to leave and join his uncle,
a Spartan general. To the Spartans,
Darius is as worthless as a mouse.
How can he prove them wrong?

Greek Tales are exciting, funny stories based
on historical events - short chapters and
illustrations throughout are perfect for
building reading confidence.

ISBN 978 0 7136 8221 2   £4.99